TARONGA

PRESENTS

BABY BOOM

ALSO IN THIS SERIES

TARONGA

PRESENTS

POO AT THE ZOO

Sophia and Ollie are zookeepers for a day . . .
cleaning up after the animals!

PARTY ANIMALS

Sophia and Ollie are zookeepers for a day . . .
and it's a celebration at Taronga Western Plains Zoo!

NIGHT OWLS

Sophia and Ollie are zookeepers for a day . . .
and a night!

TARONGA

PRESENTS

BABY BOOM

KRISTIN DARELL

Illustrated by LAURA WOOD

PENGUIN BOOKS

PENGUIN BOOKS

UK | USA | Canada | Ireland | Australia
India | New Zealand | South Africa | China

Penguin Random House Australia

Penguin Random House Australia is part of the Penguin Random House group of companies whose addresses can be found at global.penguinrandomhouse.com.

First published by Penguin Books,
an imprint of Penguin Random House Australia Pty Ltd, in 2024

Cover design by Caroline Lee © Penguin Random House Australia Pty Ltd
Author photography by Rebecca Erin Photography
Illustrator photography by Laura Wood

Printed and bound in Australia by Griffin Press, an accredited ISO AS/NZS 14001 Environmental Management Systems printer

NATIONAL LIBRARY OF AUSTRALIA
A catalogue record for this book is available from the National Library of Australia

MIX
Paper | Supporting responsible forestry
FSC www.fsc.org FSC® C018684

ISBN 978 1 76134 748 1 (Paperback)

penguin.com.au

We at Penguin Random House Australia acknowledge that Aboriginal and Torres Strait Islander peoples are the Traditional Custodians and the first storytellers of the lands on which we live and work. We honour Aboriginal and Torres Strait Islander peoples' continuous connection to Country, waters, skies and communities. We celebrate Aboriginal and Torres Strait Islander stories, traditions and living cultures; and we pay our respects to Elders past and present.

We proudly Acknowledge the Cammeraigal (Taronga Zoo, Sydney) and Wiradjuri (Taronga Western Plains Zoo, Dubbo) people, their Country, spirit and traditions as customary owners of the lands upon which our Zoos stand.

Chapter 1

Cub countdown

'Well?' Ollie demanded as Sophia skidded to a stop beside him, red-faced and puffing. 'Have they been born yet?'

He was leaning on a rake, standing on the main pathway.

'No change,' she said. 'But Mum said Kartika could go into labour any time now.'

Sophia was talking fast. Nothing got her more excited than animal babies and Taronga Zoo was having a baby boom!

She wondered how many new babies they would see this week. Lisa the chimpanzee was due to give birth, and some baby bearded dragons were expected to hatch. The meerkat pups might come out of the burrow too. But most exciting of all was Kartika, the Sumatran tiger, having her cubs. And Sophia knew that Ollie was even more excited than she was about that.

The Zoo was like their second home, and now Sophia and Ollie had their official volunteer status they got to do real jobs just like the adult volunteers. The school holidays meant they could be there every day.

Sophia and Ollie had been best friends for as long as they could remember. Sophia's mum, Donna, had been working at the Taronga Wildlife Hospital for twenty years. She started the same week Ollie's dad, Max, had got a job in the Backyard Team.

Sophia picked up a rake. 'Let's get this pathway clear so we can get back to the hospital.'

'Don't you dare, Fred!' Ollie exclaimed as a brush turkey stuck his head out of the bushes and stared at them. Then with big scratching kicks, Fred showered dirt and leaves over the clean path.

Ollie sighed. 'I just finished raking that. Not cool, Fred.'

The brush turkeys were getting ready for a baby boom too, making enormous nesting mounds out of mulch and leaves.

Fred froze again, foot raised, a black eye fixed on Ollie.

'Don't even think about it . . .'

Fred flicked his foot, sending a spray of dirt and leaves all over Ollie, then he turned and strutted away.

Sophia giggled. 'I'll clean it this time,' she said.

'Thanks.' Ollie brushed dirt and mulch from his shirt.

Sophia worked quickly, and it wasn't long before they'd stashed the rakes and were on their way to the Wildlife Hospital.

Sophia and Ollie jogged along the path and turned into the Rainforest Trail.

'Good morning, Lololi,' Sophia said, slowing to a walk as they passed the pygmy hippos. The Zoo's baby pygmy hippo was finally out in public, and mornings were the best time to see her.

She was exploring the habitat's pool, with her mum, Kambiri, at her side.

'We'll come and see you later,' Sophia said.

'Aww, Soph.' Ollie had stopped by

the fence. 'Can't we stay a little while?'

Sophia bit her lip. Lololi really was very cute. 'Okay. But not long.'

Ollie grinned. 'Did you know Lololi means "there is always love"?' he said. 'It's West African because that's the only place pygmy hippos are found in the wild.'

Ollie gave the baby hippo one last smile then started walking again.

'I wonder what they'll call Kartika's cubs?' Sophia asked.

'They'll be Indonesian names,' Ollie told her. 'That's where Sumatran tigers come from. I think she's going to have two boys and a girl.'

'I'm hoping for all girls,' Sophia said. 'But there's only a few hundred left in the wild so it doesn't really matter as long as they're healthy.'

They gave the leaf monkeys a wave and headed through the Rainforest Aviary and past Mary the sun bear, who was relaxing in her hammock.

It was still early, but there were lots of keepers and volunteers out and about getting everything ready.

'Mum said that with so many new

babies, all the keepers and vets will need lots of help,' Sophia told Ollie, as they walked up the hill behind the Taronga Food Market. 'I hope she gives us work inside the hospital. Wouldn't that be incredible? We'd be there while everything is happening.'

'Well, kinda,' Ollie said. 'But important stuff happens out here too.'

As they passed the chimpanzee habitat, Ollie pointed across to the grass where some of the Zoo's chimpanzee family were gathered. 'Lisa's baby will be born soon. And most of the animals at the Zoo give birth in their habitats, not at the hospital.'

'I know,' Sophia said. 'But when Kartika is in labour, there'll be a camera above her in the nursing box so the keepers can monitor her without interfering. And the only place to watch *that* is the Wildlife Hospital. Come on!'

She raced along the path towards the hospital. On the way, Jason, one of the reptile keepers, waved at them.

Jason had the Zoo's diamond python, Ruby, with him.

Ruby was soaking up a bit of morning sun.

'Hi, Jason,' Ollie called out, slowing down again as they passed. 'How are the dragon eggs?'

'Still eggs,' Jason said. 'But we're expecting lots of baby bearded dragons any time now. Why don't you both pop in to the Amphibian and Reptile Conservation Centre soon and have a look? You could help me out with Ruby.'

'Sounds good,' Ollie said as Sophia grabbed his elbow, gently pulling him away.

'We'll try,' Sophia said. 'But I think today's full up at the hospital.'

'You don't know that,' Ollie muttered.

Sophia pressed her lips together. 'We won't know anything if we never get there.'

'I suppose. Hi, Dad.'

Ollie's dad had just stepped out of the Backyard Team shed. He had a big box of hay in his arms.

'Hello, you two,' he said.

'Is that for Kartika's nursing box?' Ollie asked.

Max smiled. 'It sure is. Not long now until we have some more cubs to look after.'

'Let's go, Ollie.' Sophia was too excited to chat. She took off up the path and into the Wildlife Hospital.

Lani, one of the vet nurses, was just inside the door, speaking to someone they didn't know.

Sophia could hardly stand still. After what seemed like forever, Lani finally turned her way.

Even Ollie was excited now. 'Dad

had hay! Does that mean Kartika's in labour?' he burst out.

'Slow down. Not yet,' Lani said. 'The keepers are just getting everything ready.'

Suddenly, there was a clamouring of voices and fast-moving feet.

Sophia, Ollie and Lani all turned to see a vet carrying a small box disappear into one of the treatment rooms, followed by Sophia's mum. A tall man was last up the corridor, his arms full of towels.

'Eddie,' Lani called out. 'What's going on?'

'Rescued wombat joey,' he said, puffing slightly. 'And she's going to need a lot of help.'

Sophia glanced back down the corridor. 'Mum was supposed to tell us what we're doing today.'

'I'm sure she won't be too long,' Lani reassured her. 'Until then, how about you two come and help me?'

Chapter 2

Part of the job

'I never want to fold another towel again,' Ollie said, groaning.

'Or see another syringe or bottle of disinfectant,' Sophia said.

'It's all part of the job,' Lani said. 'Important too. Everything we use in the vet clinic needs to be clean, stacked and ready for when we need it.'

'There you are!'

They all looked up as Sophia's mum

walked towards them. Sophia jumped up and gave her a hug.

'They were a big help, Donna,' Lani said. 'Although you might struggle to get Sophia to clean up at home for a while.'

Donna laughed. 'You're assuming she did before.'

'Hey!' Sophia exclaimed, making them all laugh harder.

'How's the wombat joey?' Ollie asked.

'She's very young and going to need around the clock care,' Donna said. 'She wouldn't survive without her mother, but Eddie and Ingrid have hand-reared lots of babies. They know exactly what to do.'

'Is there anything we can help with?' Sophia asked.

'Not for *that* baby,' Donna replied. 'But I hope you have some raking muscles still good to go.'

Sophia and Ollie exchanged a look.

'More raking?' said Ollie, sounding disappointed. 'Please tell me it's not poo.'

Donna laughed. 'Not exactly. But I wouldn't want to spoil the surprise . . . Ahh, perfect timing.'

Standing by the door was Lars. He was loud and funny, and worked as a keeper in the Backyard to Bush precinct.

'I need some kids to help with some kids,' Lars said. He winked. 'Kids. Get it?'

Ollie was frowning.

'Not really,' said Sophia.

Lars wiggled his eyebrows. 'You'll see.'

'I thought we were raking,' Sophia said.

'You are,' he said. 'But that's not all you'll be doing. Let's get moving.'

Ollie chatted happily to Lars as they headed out of the hospital, but Sophia was still struggling to feel excited. She glanced back sadly as the hospital door closed behind her.

Sophia followed Lars and Ollie into the Backyard Team shed. A stack of hay was already piled in the back of a Taronga ute, and Jayne, another keeper, was packing and tying down buckets, feed and other equipment.

'Lars, why don't you walk with Sophia and Ollie. I'll bring the ute,' she said.

'Sounds like a plan,' Lars said.

Sophia did feel a bit happier as they headed back to the Zoo's main path. The chimpanzees had been given some breakfast, and Jimiyu, their favourite giraffe who they called Leggy, was loping slowly across the Savannah.

They had just made it to the side of the Taronga Food Market when Lars' radio crackled. Sophia and Ollie wandered over to the edge of the Asian elephant habitat as he stepped away to respond.

'Good morning, Mo!' said Ollie. 'Good morning, Boony!'

The elephants real names were Pak Boon and Tang Mo, but Sophia and Ollie called them by their nicknames.

Pak Boon was wandering towards the pond, while Tang Mo chewed happily on something.

'Lucky Boony is going to have a wash,' Lars said, joining them at the fence. 'We have a special name for elephants who never take a bath. Any ideas?'

Sophia looked at him. 'I don't know.'

'*Smelly*-phants!'

Ollie groaned. 'Your jokes are almost as bad as Pixie's.'

'I'll take that as a compliment.' Lars grinned. 'That was Pixie on the radio actually. She'll be here in just a minute.'

Sophia and Ollie both adored Pixie. She was one of the coolest people they knew. After being part of YATZ, the Youth at the Zoo program, Pixie was now volunteering, studying to be a zookeeper and working part-time in the Zoo gift shop.

'Yoo-hoo. We're here!'

Sophia spun around to say hello, but Pixie wasn't alone. Sitting on her shoulders, waving both hands wildly in the air, was Ollie's little sister, Katy.

Chapter 3

Cute kids!

'Katy!' Ollie said, looking as surprised as Sophia felt.

'Wollie!' Katy said, reaching out towards her brother.

He smiled, helping her off Pixie's shoulders and giving her a bear hug.

Sophia loved how close Ollie and Katy were. It made her wish she had a brother or sister. At least she had Ollie as a best friend, which was the next best thing.

Katy flung her arms around Sophia's legs, squeezing tight as she grinned up at her. Sophia straightened the little girl's cap. She was dressed in a Taronga Zoo t-shirt and a Taronga Zoo cap.

'Nice outfit,' Sophia said.

Katy's grin grew wider as she jumped back and did a twirl.

'Fanks,' she said.

'Why is Katy here?' asked Ollie. 'Was this what you meant by us looking after kids, Lars?'

'Nope,' he said. 'Keep guessing!'

'Your mum got called into work,' said Pixie. 'My shift at the gift shop was done. I offered to babysit so your dad didn't have to finish early.' She grinned. 'I thought you'd like to say hello.'

Katy was jumping up and down next to a large elephant statue. Sophia lifted her up, so she could swing her legs over it like she was riding a horse. Katy gave a squeal of delight.

'Absolutely,' Ollie said. He turned to Lars. 'Maybe Pixie and Katy could come with us?'

'I don't see why not,' Lars said. 'Katy will enjoy this part of the job too.'

'Awesome.' Ollie swung Katy off the elephant and onto his back. 'Let's go.'

Sophia smiled, but there was a funny tight feeling in her stomach. Ollie got to see Katy at home every day, but Sophia only got to volunteer with Ollie full-time in the holidays. She hoped having Katy there wouldn't stop them from doing grown-up jobs.

She frowned a little as she fell into step behind Pixie and Lars.

'Do you know why elephants are wrinkled?' she heard Lars say. 'It's because they're so hard to iron!'

Pixie laughed her big laugh.

'I've got a good one,' Pixie said. 'How do elephants talk to each other?'

Ollie had slowed down to listen. 'How?' he said.

'On the *ele*-phone.'

Ollie and Lars both groaned.

Everyone was chatting and laughing as they followed the trail past the camels and the Blue Mountains Bushwalk.

As Sophia walked, the feeling in her tummy eased a bit. She was with her favourite Zoo people, doing what she loved. Besides, she'd be spending the whole week working with Ollie. A couple of hours didn't matter that much.

She jogged to catch up to Ollie and Katy. Ollie had put his sister down and she was pretending to fly, arms outstretched like a bird they had seen as they passed the Aviary.

'Okay, you lot,' Lars said. They had arrived at Backyard to Bush. It was busy with families now that the Zoo was open. 'Sophia and Ollie, we're heading to the Farm Yard. Pixie, why don't you and Katy meet us there in half an hour?'

'Will do,' Pixie said. She crouched down in front of Katy. 'Want to go see a quokka?'

Katy clapped happily.

'You two, this way,' Lars said, leading Sophia and Ollie along the trail. Sophia's spirits lifted as they wove their way through the crowds.

Lars stopped in front of the barn. 'I have a question for you,' he said. 'What do goats have for breakfast?'

Sophia's eyes narrowed. 'Is this a test or another joke?'

Lars just smiled.

Sophia sighed. 'I don't know,' she said.

'*Goat*-meal.'

Ollie was grinning, and Sophia couldn't help giggling a bit.

Her laugh turned into a gasp as Lars opened the door to the barn and gestured them inside.

'Oh, my goodness,' she squeaked out. 'When you said kids you meant baby goats!'

They raced inside, crouching to peer through the gaps between the timbers of a fence. Inside, wobbling and hopping around were two tiny goats.

'They're SO cute,' Sophia said.

One of the kids stumbled its way to the fence in front of Sophia and Ollie.

'They're only one week old,' said Lars. 'That's Timmy. You can pat him if you like. The other little one there is Tommy.'

Ollie's grin was huge. 'Hey, buddy.'

Sophia reached out to Timmy and he started nuzzling her hand.

‘These guys arrived a bit earlier than we thought,’ said Lars, ‘and we need to get this old hay out and the new stuff down. Then you can have some time with them before we open the barn.’

Sophia stood up. ‘Let’s get to work.’

Chapter 4

Kid care

Sophia and Ollie were sweaty and dirty by the time they'd finished clearing out the pen. Pixie and Katy arrived in the barn just as they started replacing the hay.

Katy was so excited to see the baby goats. Pixie was doubled over laughing as the little girl copied every jump, hop and stumble the kids made.

Finally, the new hay was in place.

Tired, but happy, Sophia and Ollie sat down, leaning against a timber post.

Tommy wobbled over to Sophia, plonking down and resting his head on her leg. His ears were huge and soft, and the look on his little face was so much like a smile that she grinned back.

Katy had finally been allowed inside the fenced area. She ran straight to Ollie.

'Katy, you need to sit down,' he said, in his patient big-brother voice.

She slowly sank to the hay, and Ollie sat next to her.

'Now, remember . . .' He raised a finger to his lips.

'Shhh,' Katy said, copying him.

Timmy had been hovering near his mum, but came over to see what was happening. He took some little steps towards Katy. She started wiggling, but Sophia could see how hard she was trying to be still and quiet.

Timmy moved towards her, sniffing her arm and rubbing his head against her hand. Katy giggled.

'You can give him a gentle pat if he'll let you,' Lars said.

Katy carefully stroked Timmy and, for a moment, the kid rested his head on her shoulder.

Then Timmy was off, bouncing and jumping around again. Tommy took off too, and Sophia and Ollie stood up.

'We're going to open the barn up now,' Lars told them. 'Thank you so much for your help. Donna said to tell you that your jobs are done for the day so you can help out anyone who needs you or just hang out.'

'We're going for some lunch, aren't we, Katy?' Pixie said. 'How about you guys come too? My shout.'

'Chippies?' Katy said, hope in her eyes.

'Maybe.' Pixie smiled. 'But other things too.'

'Sounds great,' Ollie said. 'Right, Soph?'

The tightness in Sophia's tummy was back, but she nodded. She had to eat lunch at some stage. After that it would just be her and Ollie again, and they could get back to the Wildlife Hospital.

Katy had decided she was now a baby goat and answered every question with a little *baaaa*.

On the way, they took a detour to visit the lemurs. They were swinging around in their habitat and talking to each other with loud shrieking calls.

When Katy stopped for a play at the Forest Adventure Playground, she decided she was a baby lemur and did the same.

'Careful, Katy!' Ollie stayed really close to his sister to make sure she didn't go too high.

'He's such a good big brother,' Pixie said, coming to stand beside Sophia.

Sophia didn't say anything.

'Are you okay?'

'Huh? Yeah, course,' Sophia said.

'Okay.' Pixie's eyes narrowed a little, like she didn't believe her. 'Time to go, baby lemur,' she called out to Katy.

Katy responded with a piercing lemur shriek.

Ollie laughed. 'That's horrible! Let's hope she's not pretending to be a lemur for long.'

They stopped and said hello to Mackenzie the cassowary and the capybaras next to the playground. Ollie shook his head at the giant rodents. He still hadn't forgiven them after learning they ate their own poo.

Sophia stayed quiet as they walked the rest of the way up to the main entrance plaza and the cafe. She couldn't stop thinking about the rescued wombat joey. Her mum had fostered lots of baby animals before, but they had never had a wombat baby to look after.

She was keen to head back to the Wildlife Hospital but knew Ollie wouldn't go until Max finished his shift and took Katy home.

They ordered some lunch and sat in the shade. The Zoo was busy, but over the hum of voices, they could still hear the calls of hundreds of birds. Sophia looked up and saw one of the Zoo's cheeky wild kookaburras eyeing them.

'Where's my little monkey?' Max said, striding around the tables.

'Not monkey,' Katy said, jumping up and running over to him. '*Koo-koo-koo-kaa-kaa-kaa*.'

'Okay, then,' he said, grinning. 'My little kookaburra, it is! Thanks for your help today, Pixie. Before I forget. I have some news. Kartika's been checking out the nursing box.'

Sophia jumped up. 'What? Oh, my goodness. Are there any cubs yet? Are they all okay?'

'Whoa, whoa, whoa,' Max said.

'I don't think she's in labour yet.'

Sophia packed up the remains of her lunch. She had to get back to the Wildlife Hospital *now* to find out more news!

'Soph,' Max continued. 'Your mum said to see if you want to come home with us. She's not sure when she'll be able to get away and your dad can't pick you up for a few hours.'

Leave? No way. Why would she want to leave when Kartika might be having her cubs?

'Thanks, Max, but I'm happy to stay here.' Sophia turned to Ollie, grinning. 'Ready to head back down?'

Ollie was holding Katy's hand and chewing on his lip.

'Well . . .' he said.

Sophia's smile faded as she looked at him. 'What's wrong?' she asked. 'Kartika might be having her babies. We need to get going.'

'She probably won't have them today,' Ollie said. 'She hasn't even gone into labour yet.'

Sophia's heart started to race. She didn't understand. Ollie knew that Zoo things weren't the same if they weren't together. Together was how it was supposed to be.

'I think I'll go home with Dad and Katy,' Ollie said quietly. 'That's okay, right? You don't mind?'

Sophia cleared her throat and forced a small smile. 'Sure,' she said. 'All good. See you in the morning. Bye, everyone.'

Then she turned and walked quickly away, before any of them could see how upset she was.

Chapter 5

Rescue!

Sophia made her way back to the Wildlife Hospital. She found Lani cleaning up in one of the treatment rooms and was about to ask her a million questions about tiger births when they were interrupted by worried voices outside.

Sophia walked to the door and peered out. Four people were carrying a large black tub down the corridor. They turned into one of the other rooms.

'Another animal's been brought in,' she told Lani. 'But I can't see what. It's in a big tub.'

'I'd better go and see if they need help,' Lani said, hurrying out the door.

Sophia couldn't resist. She only waited a moment before following and peering through the door's viewing window.

'Oh, wow,' Sophia said under her breath.

The nurses had just lifted a small long-nosed fur seal onto a covered table. It wasn't moving.

Lani, Sophia's mum and the senior vet, Lauren, were in the room too.

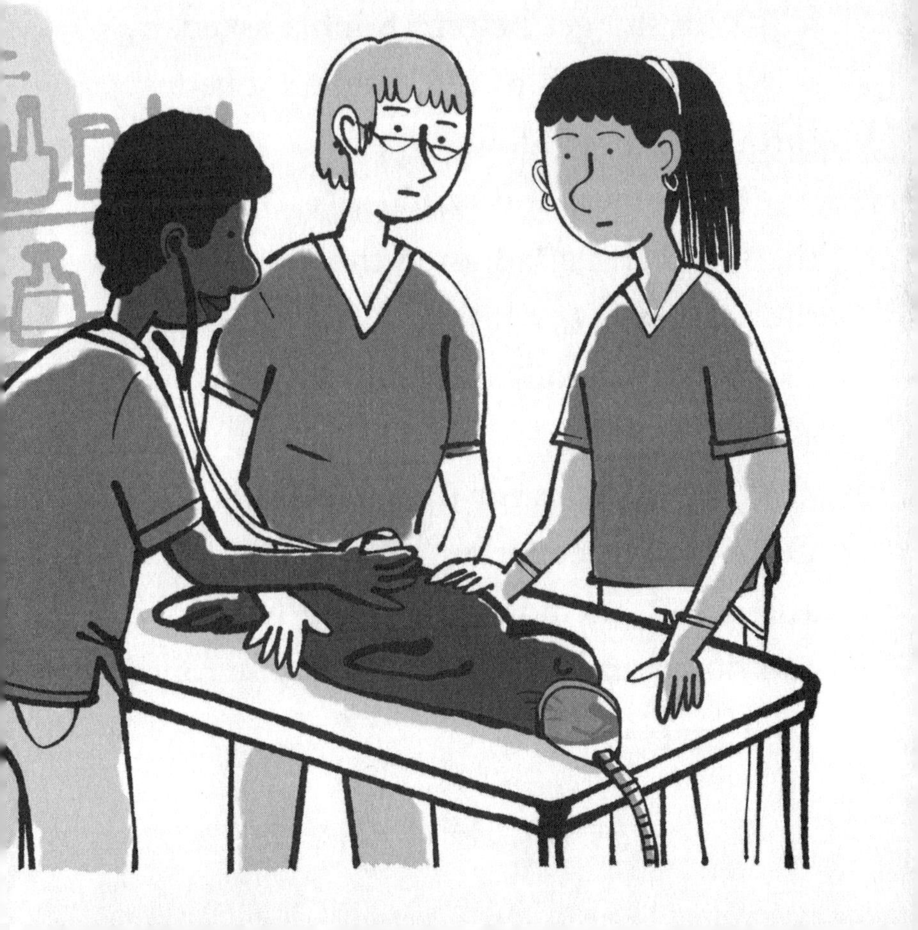

Sophia turned to see Eddie walking up the corridor, holding what looked like a beanie gently in his arms. Inside would be the wombat joey.

'That poor little seal,' he said. 'I heard them saying she hadn't eaten in quite a while before she was brought in.'

'Will she get better?' Sophia asked.

'It's too soon to tell.' Eddie looked through the window.

They stood and watched as one of the hospital staff adjusted the mask on the seal's sweet, whiskered face.

'What are they doing now?' Sophia asked.

'That mask is for the anaesthetic. Once she's asleep, they'll do a full assessment, including checking her blood and doing an X-ray to see what's wrong,' Eddie explained.

'I had an X-ray once,' Sophia said, looking at the little seal. 'I'd broken my arm. Turns out I couldn't fly after all.'

Eddie chuckled. He looked back through the window. 'Between Taronga's Wildlife Hospitals, here and at Dubbo, we treat around one thousand five hundred animals every year,' he said. 'And that's not including the help we give the animals at the Zoos.'

'That's a lot,' Sophia said. She was surprised, but it also made her more determined than ever to be a vet one day and do her bit.

'Can I do anything to help?' Sophia asked.

'Not for the seal,' Eddie said. 'They'll handle it as little as possible because it's wild and they'll want to release it as soon as it's well. Our wombat joey is awake, though. Do you want a little peek?'

Sophia nodded and stepped closer.

'Oh!' She sucked in her breath as a little head appeared.

'We're calling her Waddle the wombat,' Eddie said. 'Cute, huh?'

Waddle had pink skin with a soft covering of light grey fur and huge ears. She also had the cutest nose Sophia had ever seen.

'Hey, Waddle,' Sophia said. 'You're going to be just fine.'

The little joey blinked its eyes a couple of times, and Sophia felt like her heart was stretching with love. She knew she was very lucky to be there.

'Eddie,' Sophia said. 'Is there anything I can do to help you? I'm hanging around anyway.'

'That would be brilliant,' he said. 'It's time for a feed. You can mix the formula for me.'

Sophia was so nervous as she carefully weighed out the formula, made specially for Waddle.

'It's full of all the good things she

needs to grow into a big healthy wombat,' Eddie said.

Next, he told Sophia how to transfer the formula to a bottle and add some special milk powder and water. She gave it a good shake.

'Baby wombats need about ten to fifteen per cent of their body weight in milk every day,' Eddie explained, as she handed him the bottle. 'That's why they have to feed so often.'

Sophia sat down to watch as Eddie repositioned Waddle to feed her. He was cradling the little joey so it could suck on the bottle, just like Ollie's mum and dad used to do with Katy.

'I wish Ollie was here to see this,' she said, as the little joey chugged down her milk.

'I know you're best friends,' Eddie said. 'But I've noticed this vet stuff seems to be more your thing than Ollie's. If you two keep working here, you'll probably end up in different areas of the Zoo. It doesn't mean you can't still be friends. You'll just have twice the experiences to share.'

Sophia thought about that a moment, then she smiled.

Eddie was right. She glanced at Waddle. Instead of feeling sad, now she was excited to tell Ollie all about it.

She felt a bit embarrassed that she'd been so upset about Ollie leaving and about having Katy around. Sure, it meant they hadn't been able to help out as much as they could have without her there, but in the end, it hadn't mattered. And family was important.

She was here in Taronga's Wildlife Hospital. She was even doing real hospital jobs. She promised herself to be different if the same thing happened again.

Chapter 6

Roo poo!

'Soph, are you sure you're okay about yesterday?' Ollie asked her the next day. They'd just finished their rounds, clearing the pathways.

Sophia thought about it. She really was. She nodded. 'Yep!'

As they headed back to the Wildlife Hospital, she told Ollie all about what had happened after he left.

'That sounds like your perfect day!'

Ollie said when she'd finished.

Sophia grinned. 'It really was.'

They walked the rest of the way in silence, the chirps and caws of the birds echoing around the still empty Zoo.

They were just outside the hospital when Ollie stopped. 'Soph?' he said.

'Yeah. What's up?'

'When you said you were okay about yesterday, you meant about me leaving but also about Katy being here with us, right?' Ollie asked.

'Sure,' Sophia said.

Ollie let out a big breath. 'Awesome. Because Mum got another last-minute work shift, so Katy's coming back to the Zoo today,' he said. 'At lunch. Just for a few hours,' he added quickly.

Sophia ignored the disappointed twinge in her tummy. 'All good!' she said firmly. At least they had until lunchtime.

They found Sophia's mum in a hospital treatment room with Eddie. He had the orphaned wombat joey snuggled deep inside the pouch on his lap. His mouth opened in an enormous yawn.

'Eddie's had a long night taking care of this little joey,' Donna said, as they walked into the room.

'Yeah,' Eddie said. 'She's feeding every four hours, plus toilet stops. We make it *most* of the time. When we don't . . .' Eddie winced. 'There's a bit of clean up. Picture squishy browny-green cubes . . .'

'I'd rather not,' Ollie said, quickly.

Everyone laughed.

'Ingrid will be here soon to take over,' Donna said. 'Eddie, make sure you get some rest.'

'Thanks,' Eddie said. 'Sophia did

a great job making the joey's food yesterday. I'll tell Ingrid she can call on her if she needs help.'

Donna smiled proudly, and Sophia's cheeks felt hot.

'Right, Ollie and Soph,' Donna said. 'Ben asked if you could help him clean over in buru nura – Kangaroo Country.'

'Sure!' Ollie said, even as Sophia's shoulders slumped a little.

'Come on, Soph,' Ollie said. 'It'll be fun.'

Sophia nodded. She didn't say much on the walk to Nura Diya Australia. She was battling with her own brain. She didn't mind doing jobs, but today she'd been dying to spend more time at the hospital before Katy got there and they had to babysit.

She took another deep breath, determined to stay in a good mood.

Ben was waiting for them at the kangaroos.

'I hear you've been doing amazing things,' he said. 'I was out at Dubbo last week and Petra showed me your echidna enrichment design for Smudge. Very impressive.'

'That was mostly Ollie's work,' Sophia said.

'Not true,' Ollie said, laughing. 'You put in the maggots.'

Sophia shuddered at the memory.

Even though they were cleaning up poo again, Sophia did have fun. It didn't seem so icky anymore and there was so much happening. The kangaroos were so curious and cute, and there were even three cute kangaroo joeys hopping around.

'This one is so tiny,' Sophia said, as a curious joey sniffed at her shoe. She patted its back. 'And so soft.'

'That kanga has a wonky ear,' Ollie said. 'Katy will love it!'

'That's a great idea. We can bring Katy to see them,' Sophia said, determined to stay positive. 'And kangaroos make quiet noises. We don't want her to be a lemur again!'

'True,' Ollie replied with a grin.

Ollie held up the bucket of kangaroo poo. 'Hey, Ben. What's happening with this?'

'It's going to Rohan, for the lions,' Ben said.

'We can take it,' Sophia said quickly. 'We're going back to the Wildlife Hospital, and it's almost on the way.'

Ben gave them two thumbs up.

Sophia and Ollie carried the bucket back along the main path, weaving through the holiday crowds.

Sophia waved at some kids, who were shyly whispering and pointing. Sophia always felt so proud when other kids realised she was working at the Zoo.

They waved back and ran off giggling.

It was nice to see Maya, Ato and their lion cubs, but getting back to the hospital was the priority.

As soon as they stepped through the doors at the Wildlife Hospital it was clear something was going on.

'Do you think Kartika is having her cubs?' Ollie asked.

'It could be anything,' Sophia said, trying not to get her hopes up. She spotted her mum coming out of a room.

'Mum, what's going on?' Sophia's heart was racing. 'Is it the cubs?'

Her mum was grinning at them, but she shook her head. 'No,' she said. 'Although the keepers think she's close.'

'What is it then?' Sophia asked.

Donna's grin grew wider. 'The meerkat babies are out of the burrow and you two are going to help.'

Chapter 7

Meerkat mayhem

Sophia's hands flew to her mouth. She loved all the animals, but the meerkats were her favourites. Meerkat pups! She could hardly believe it.

Donna shooed them back out the hospital door. 'Amane and John are waiting for you in the Backyard Team shed. You've got a quick stop to make first.'

The meerkat keepers were sitting in one of the Zoo's buggies.

'How are our helpers today?' John asked.

'So excited,' Sophia said.

'Thanks for letting us come along,' Ollie said, as they all climbed into the cart.

'We just have to pick up some meerkat snacks first and then you'll have the best job in the Zoo,' Amane said, smiling over her shoulder.

Sophia couldn't sit still as they wound their way around until they arrived at another building.

'This way,' John said. He led them through a door and into an enormous room.

There were boxes full of food stacked up everywhere, people at metal benches, chopping and sorting and weighing things, and a whole wall of huge doors. Sophia figured they must be fridges or freezers. It was the biggest kitchen she'd ever seen.

'Sophia. Ollie.' Amane was waving them over to a bench where the Zoo's nutritionist, Meica, was chatting with John.

'How much do you know about what meerkats eat?' Meica asked them.

'Mostly insects?' Ollie said.

'And sometimes eggs, fruit and plants too?' Sophia added.

'Very good,' Meica said. 'But there's one insect that's such a treat it's like chocolate for meerkats. Any ideas?'

Sophia and Ollie shook their heads.

'I have some here,' Meica said.

She was holding a little container.

Meica lifted the lid.

Sophia's stomach lurched and she could see Ollie trying hard not to laugh. Inside the container were squirmy, wiggly, writhing mealworms.

She hated maggots most of all, and mealworms looked a lot like them. At least they didn't *smell* like maggots, she noticed with relief.

'Sophia is great with bugs.' Ollie's eyes were twinkling.

'Brilliant,' Amane said. 'You can carry them, Soph.'

'Awesome,' Sophia said in a tone that said it really wasn't.

Ollie finally gave up trying not to laugh.

The area outside the meerkat habitat was packed. Sophia tried to get a glimpse of the pups, but there were too many people in the way.

'Over here,' Amane said. She led Ollie and Sophia around one side and through a gate.

Now Sophia could see the whole habitat, and she could barely breathe with happiness. Four meerkat pups were scurrying around, digging in the dirt and chasing each other. They looked just like the grown-up meerkats, but miniature.

One pup tried standing on its hind legs, then toppled sideways.

'They're adorable,' she said. 'And slightly uncoordinated.'

'Are they trying to be lookouts like the grown ups?' Ollie asked, as another pup stood on its back legs, then tumbled over.

John nodded. 'They start copying the adults early to learn,' he explained while three of the pups rolled and tumbled on top of each other. He laughed. 'With mixed results as you can see.'

'Let's get them fed,' Amane said.

'How?' Ollie asked.

'You'll take food in of course.'

'Do you mean *us*?' Sophia asked. 'Actually feeding them?' Sophia looked at Ollie.

'WOW,' he mouthed silently.

'We've put a hold on meerkat encounters until the pups have grown a bit,' John explained. 'We thought you two might like to help with conditioning the pups to being around humans.'

Amane handed Sophia and Ollie each a container. Sophia opened the container and winced. She'd forgotten about the mealworms.

'Just sit on the rock and scatter the food around you,' Amane said. 'They'll come to you.'

'No problem,' Sophia said.

As soon as Sophia and Ollie sat down, they were surrounded by meerkats.

The meerkats clearly loved the mealworms. The moment one landed on the ground a meerkat was there to munch it down.

They were scurrying all around Sophia and Ollie, climbing over their legs to get to the food.

Sophia's heart felt like it might explode with joy.

Sophia and Ollie's eyes met. They didn't need to say anything. This was incredible.

The pups had held back but were now coming to investigate. One had run over Ollie's lap and was sitting there inspecting him, his black nose sniffing the air.

Sophia felt something leaning against her arm, but she didn't dare move. Then that something tickled her!

Ollie laughed. 'You make a good lookout location,' he said.

Sophia glanced sideways. A meerkat was standing sentry next to her, leaning on her arm, his pointy little face tilted up at her, and a pup had now made itself comfortable in her lap. She grinned, trying desperately not to move.

She never wanted this moment to end.

When all the food was eaten and all the meerkats were back on the ground, Sophia and Ollie stood up.

Neither of them could speak. No words seemed enough.

They reluctantly headed back to the gate. Ollie grinned and started chatting to the kids who were lining up along the glass edge of the enclosure. They were smiling up at him, excited looks on their faces.

'Thank you so much,' Sophia said to the keepers.

'We all work hard,' John said. 'But days like this definitely make it worthwhile.'

Ollie and Sophia headed back around to the outside of the habitat. They found a space and leaned on the rail.

Sophia was sure this had to be the best day of her life. She never wanted to leave.

'Oh, crackers,' Ollie said suddenly. 'Mum's dropping Katy soon. I said I'd meet her and Pixie up at the gift shop.'

Sophia hesitated, looking from Ollie to the meerkats and back.

'You can stay here if you like,' he said.

Sophia knew he would be fine with that. But she also knew Ollie wanted her to come along.

'It's okay,' she said. 'Let's go.'

Chapter 8

Tiger trek

'Last one, Katy,' Pixie said. She was carrying a big box with toy giraffes and koalas poking out the top.

Sophia and Ollie had made it to the gift shop just as Ollie's mum, Siobhan, arrived with Katy, but Pixie hadn't quite finished work.

'Katy, put that back, please,' Ollie said.

When Katy saw Pixie putting toys on the shelves, she'd wanted to help. The only problem was, she was taking things *off* the shelves. She was being so cute that it was hard to tell her to stop. Plus, she was dressed like a tiger with ears and a tail, and painted-on whiskers.

Sophia's stomach was hurting from giggling, as Ollie patiently took another stack of toy animals out of Katy's arms.

The crowd of people who had stopped to watch her was almost as big as the crowd watching the meerkats.

'Look, Katy,' Pixie said, pulling something out of the box. 'A tiger, like you.'

'*Grrr*,' she said.

Pixie laughed. 'Well, I'm finally finished, no thanks to you, Katy,' she said. 'Where do you lot want to go after lunch?'

'*Grrr*,' Katy said again, grabbing Pixie's hand.

'Okay,' Pixie said. 'Tiger Trek it is.'

They all loved the entry to Tiger Trek. It was designed to look like the inside of a plane so you could pretend you were flying to Sumatra in Indonesia. Sophia hoped one day she'd get to fly there for real.

Ollie already knew all about why the Sumatran tigers are critically endangered. Once, he'd sat there while the video played three times, writing everything in his Fun Fact File. Today they only listened to it once.

Once inside, the three of them followed Katy around the next corner. In front of them was a high glass wall with a jeep sticking mostly through the glass. When you climbed inside the front seat you were in the tiger habitat. It was like driving in the wild surrounded by tigers!

Sophia and Ollie climbed quickly inside the jeep.

Ollie gasped – Clarence, Kartika's partner, jumped up and was walking towards them over the top of the bonnet.

Then he was looking straight into the front window!

Clarence stared at them with his wide golden eyes then jumped down and stalked off.

'Look, there's Kembali, Kartika's brother, over on that raised timber platform,' Ollie said.

The Zoo's tigers were some of Ollie's favourite animals, and he could always recognise them faster than Sophia could.

As they walked around the Tiger Trek, Ollie seemed lost in thought.

'You two are very quiet,' Pixie said. 'Right, I've got a joke for you.'

'Oh dear,' Sophia said.

'Why are tigers terrible storytellers?' Pixie opened her eyes really wide.

'Why?' Sophia asked.

'Because they only have one *tail*! Get it? Tale?'

'That was actually pretty funny,' Sophia said.

Pixie crossed her arms, her mouth open in mock shock. 'You don't have to sound so surprised.'

But Ollie was still lost in thought.

'I can't see Kartika! Let's check around here,' he said finally, heading further around the habitat.

Sophia looked at Ollie.

'Are you thinking what I'm thinking?' he asked.

Sophia nodded. 'Maybe! I'm thinking if Kartika's not here, that might mean . . .'

'She's in her nursing box, in labour,' Ollie finished. 'Let's find out.'

Pixie grinned. 'It's almost time to drop Katy to Max. Let's go and see if we have any new mums at the Zoo today.'

Sophia and Ollie led the way. Sophia glanced quickly into the chimpanzee habitat. Lisa was there munching on some vegetables. No new baby there. Sophia wondered if the bearded dragon eggs had hatched yet. She made a mental note to check later.

Holding Katy's hand, Pixie headed in the direction of the Backyard Team shed, while Sophia and Ollie raced straight through the Wildlife Hospital doors.

They spotted Lani first. Her face said it all.

She took their hands, grinning. 'It's happening!' she said. 'Follow me.'

Chapter 9

It's happening!

Lani led Sophia and Ollie down the corridor. She paused at a door. Sophia's mum was sitting in the chair right in front of a monitor. From the doorway, they could just make out a black-and-white image moving on the screen.

'That must be Kartika right now,' Ollie said quietly.

'Wow,' Sophia said.

A lady with glasses was standing in

the corridor behind them holding a steaming cup of tea. It was Marwa, one of the carnivore keepers.

'Come in and have a closer look,' she said.

Ollie sucked in a little breath. 'Really?'

'Really,' Marwa said with a smile.

They followed her into the room. Donna stood up when she saw Marwa.

'No change,' Donna said.

'Thanks.' Marwa took the seat in front of the monitor. She waved Sophia and Ollie closer.

Now they could clearly see Kartika lying on hay in her nursing box.

'Kartika's resting now, but see how she's panting – that means her labour has started.' Marwa explained. 'Tiger labour can last twelve hours!'

Ollie peered closer at the monitor. 'Do you think she'll take that long?'

'We've no idea,' Marwa said. 'It's up to Kartika now.'

The tiger stood up, her fur rippling as she circled the space. Sophia held her breath. Was a cub coming already?

Kartika took a few more steps, then re-settled herself back in the hay. Sophia exhaled.

'Will you be okay for a while, Marwa?' Donna asked.

'Absolutely fine,' she said. 'I'll call you if there are any dramas, and Brad's going to relieve me in a few hours.'

'Great,' Donna said, turning to face Sophia and Ollie. 'You two can come with me.'

'But . . .' Sophia started to argue.

Her mum raised her eyebrows.

'Okay, Mum.' Sophia looked longingly at the screen.

'Pop back in anytime,' Marwa said. 'We could be here a while.'

'It's incredible,' Ollie said as they followed Donna outside the Wildlife Hospital. 'Just think, by tomorrow there will be more Sumatran tigers in the world. That's so insanely cool.'

'WOLLIE!' Katy came racing towards them, tiger tail flying out behind.

She leapt into Ollie's arms. Then she grinned at Sophia and blew her a kiss. Sophia smiled back.

'Hi, Max. Hi, Pixie,' Donna said.

'Any cubs yet?' Pixie asked.

Donna shook her head. 'But Kartika's looking good, so . . .' She held up crossed fingers.

Pixie did the same with both hands and crossed her legs. They laughed as Pixie stumbled and almost fell.

'I'm ready to head off,' Max said. 'I think this tiger cub needs a nap.'

Katy was now snuggled into Ollie's shoulder, her painted-on whiskers all smudged and her eyes almost shut.

'Max has offered to drop you home, Soph,' Donna said. 'With everything going on, I'm not sure what time I'll be leaving.'

Sophia was shaking her head. 'Please, please, Mum, can we stay?' She glanced quickly at Ollie, realising she'd automatically included him. 'I mean, can I stay, and Ollie, if he wants to.'

Her mum didn't answer straight away. Sophia took that as a good sign.

'We won't get in the way. I mean, I won't get in the way.' Her eyes darted to Ollie again. 'Please.'

'I guess it isn't every day Sumatran

tiger cubs are born,' Donna said.

Sophia let out a little squeal. That was a yes!

'Thank you, Mum! Thank you.'

She turned to Ollie. He loved tigers so much. Surely he would want to stay for this? Katy was now fast asleep on his shoulder.

'Ollie?' Sophia asked.

He was chewing his lip. He looked quickly at Katy. 'She looks pretty comfy. I think I should go with Dad and–'

'Sure, fine, no worries,' Sophia said, interrupting him. 'See you later.' She spun and raced back inside.

Once she was through the door, she paused. She tried to remember that it had been great spending time on her own yesterday and Ollie had enjoyed hearing about it. But even though she'd promised herself to be okay, she still felt sad. Ollie was her best friend.

She walked into the back room. There was a huge bundle of clean towels piled in a basket. She sat down and got to work folding them.

'Finally. There you are.'

Sophia's head snapped up at the sound of Ollie's voice.

'What are you doing here?' she asked, surprised. 'I thought–'

'You didn't let me finish what I was going to say.' He sounded a little bit annoyed. 'I was trying to tell you I needed to help Dad get Katy to the car, because she'd fallen asleep on me. But then I'd be back.'

‘Oh.’ Sophia screwed up her nose.

Ollie sighed. ‘As if I wouldn’t want to stay, Soph. I mean . . . tigers cubs!’ He was smiling now. ‘Besides, I know how much this vet stuff means to you.’

Sophia smiled now too. ‘Sorry.’

‘It’s okay.’ He looked up at the towering pile in front of her. ‘That’s a lot of towels.’

Sophia shrugged. ‘I didn’t know what else to do.’

‘Well, I do,’ Ollie said. ‘Pixie wants us to tag along with her. She’s promised we’ll know as soon as something happens up here, and then we can head straight back.’

‘Where are we going?’ Sophia asked.

Ollie’s eyes lit up with excitement. ‘You have to guess.’

Chapter 10

A shower surprise

'Zebras?' Sophia asked.

'Nope,' Ollie replied.

'Gorillas?'

'Nope.'

'Sun bear? Tortoise?'

'No and no!'

'Hrmph.' Sophia pressed her lips together and kept walking.

Ever since they'd picked up a bucket of leafy greens, Sophia had been trying to work out which animal they were visiting.

Now they were following the main path right around the edge of the Zoo.

'Is it bongos?' she said suddenly.

'No.'

A smile spread across Sophia's face. 'Lololi,' she said.

Ollie's smile told her she'd got it right.

'Hi, Pixie!' Ollie called out, as they turned into the Rainforest Trail.

'Hey. Thanks for grabbing the greens,' she said.

'No worries.' Ollie handed her the bucket. 'It was good of you to *lettuce* help.'

Pixie cackled. 'My pleasure. It was

good of you to *turnip*.' She paused. 'Get it? Turn ip . . . Turn up!'

Sophia groaned. 'You two and Lars are all as bad as each other.'

'Follow me.' Pixie led them into the staff-only area behind the pygmy hippo habitat.

Paul, an ungulate keeper, was crouched down at the edge of an open space. There was a divider between him and where the hippos were.

Kambiri was standing quite close to Paul with Lololi at her side. The calf was snuffling around happily, while her mum stood calmly nearby.

Sophia and Ollie exchanged excited looks. They'd never been this close to the pygmy hippos before.

'Welcome to the exclusive pygmy hippo spa,' Paul said.

'What do you mean "spa"?' Sophia asked.

Paul picked up a hose and turned it on. 'We're going to give these two a shower.'

'No way,' Ollie said. 'That's so cool.'

'Actually, it will be warm,' Paul said, laughing.

Pixie threw Kambiri and Lololi a handful of greens and they started munching away.

'We're going to see what these two would like best,' Paul explained. 'They can choose whether they want a snack or a shower. Pixie, why don't you show Soph what to do, then she can have a go.'

Pixie took the hose from Paul and pointed it towards the hippos, letting the water fall in front of Kambiri.

Kambiri looked up and then walked through the stream of water. Pixie moved the water back and forth across her back.

'Your turn, Soph,' Pixie said. 'You can see if Lololi wants a shower, too, if you like.'

'Yes, please! If I were a hippo, I'd think this was pretty nice,' Sophia said.

'Do you get to do this every day?' Ollie asked Paul, as Sophia took the hose and let the water fall near Lololi.

Paul nodded. 'Pygmy hippos aren't in the water all the time, unlike the bigger common hippos.'

'So that's why a pygmy hippo's eyes can be on the sides rather than the top of its head!' said Ollie.

'Huh?' said Sophia, trying to remember what common hippos looked like. 'I never thought to ask why they were different.'

'Common hippos are in the water so much, but they still need to look out for danger,' Ollie said. 'So their eyes have to be above the water, even when the rest of them isn't.'

Paul looked impressed.

'Watch out, Paul,' Pixie said. 'Ollie will be doing your keeper talks soon if you're not careful.'

But now Sophia was only half listening. She was in her happy place and she could see little Lololi was enjoying herself too.

Kambiri was munching happily on lettuce, watching Lololi let the water run over her.

'Okay,' Paul said. 'Sophia, keep the shower going for Lololi. Ollie, I could use your help over here. I've heard you've made some enrichment activities for an echidna and you've taken koala poo to the lions to play around with?'

Ollie nodded and Paul handed him some more greens.

'Well, you're going to love the enrichment puzzle I made for these guys,' he said.

Paul walked over to the wall and picked up a big, round container with holes in it.

He asked Ollie to put the rest of the greens into the container. And then helped him to roll it into the habitat.

Kambiri looked very interested. She wandered towards them. She was really close now. So close that Ollie could have reached out to touch her. His face was pink with excitement.

'Her skin looks quite bumpy,' Ollie said, surprised.

'They're pores,' Pixie explained. 'Hippos don't sweat, but they have natural sunscreen. When they're hot and out of the water, a clear liquid comes up through the pores to protect their skin.'

Sophia looked closely at Lololi, noticing the texture of her skin. She could see what Pixie meant. Lololi's skin was tough and textured and bumpy, like a basketball.

Kambiri loved the puzzle. She rolled it and hooked her big mouth around it, working hard to get the tasty greens out.

‘That was absolutely, insanely, amazing,’ Sophia said as they headed back along the Rainforest Trail.

Pixie was grinning. ‘Yeah, I thought you might like it.’ She glanced back towards the pygmy hippo habitat. ‘I’d never thought of working in that area before. But hippos are really growing on me.’

‘I love hippos too,’ Ollie said. ‘Almost as much as tigers.’

They all stopped and looked at each other. While they’d been with the pygmy hippos, Sophia hadn’t even thought about Kartika. Now she was desperate to know if the cubs had been born.

Pixie contacted Marwa on the radio.

'Marwa said there aren't any cubs yet,' Pixie told them, 'but Kartika's getting up and down a lot more. She's definitely close. I've got to head back to close up the shop. Let's get Marwa a treat on the way. I think there might be a bit of a celebration soon.'

'Absolutely,' Sophia said.

'Let's go,' Ollie said. 'I'm going to get the choc-honeycomb squares. They're tiger colours!'

They took off at a run.

Chapter 11

Little bundles

Sophia, Ollie and Pixie headed straight to the room where Marwa was watching Kartika.

They were almost at the door when they heard Marwa cry out. They ran the final few steps and dumped their treats in a pile on a bench. Marwa was on her feet, her hands to her mouth.

'She's had one,' Marwa said.

Sophia and Ollie moved closer to the

screen as Marwa spoke quickly on the radio. The black-and-white image showed Kartika gently licking a tiny little bundle of fur lying near her front paws.

Sophia glanced at Ollie. He had a huge smile on his face. She squeezed his hand. She knew how much this meant to him.

People were coming in and out of the room now, wanting a glimpse of the cub as they got on with work.

'Where's Mum?' Sophia asked. 'She wouldn't want to miss this.'

'She's in surgery,' Marwa said. 'They have a full list. Later they'll be operating on the seal pup that was brought in yesterday.'

'Oh.' Sophia felt worried. Something must have been really wrong with the little seal. 'What will you do if Kartika needs a vet?'

'It's okay,' Marwa said. 'Kartika's birthed this little one with no problem at all, and we won't need the vets unless there's cause for concern. Let's hope the rest go just as well.'

'How many cubs do you think she'll have?' Ollie asked.

‘Three,’ Marwa told him. ‘So, there’s still a way to go.’

‘Break out the honeycomb chocs!’ said Ollie.

‘Yum,’ Marwa said, crunching into a square. ‘This was a good idea.’

Ollie did the same. ‘So good,’ he said.

Sophia preferred to nibble the chocolate off hers before crunching into the honeycomb. It was delicious. She hadn’t realised how hungry she was.

They were laughing and chatting when suddenly Marwa’s body went tense.

‘Look,’ she said.

Kartika was circling the nursing box. Suddenly a shape dropped onto the hay. The tiger settled down again and began licking another tiny cub. The first cub wiggled over to its mum’s belly and settled in for a drink.

'Wow,' Sophia said quietly.

Sophia, Ollie and Marwa had another piece of honeycomb each to celebrate.

It was amazing how quickly time passed as they watched Kartika cleaning and caring for her two cubs. A whole hour went by as Sophia and Ollie chatted with Marwa.

'Why are they operating on the little seal?' Sophia asked, her thoughts returning to the pup.

Marwa frowned. 'There was plastic in her stomach,' she said. 'Unfortunately, that happens a lot.'

'Can't they just poop it out?' Sophia asked.

'Not always,' Marwa said. 'The plastic does all sorts of damage inside and can stop them being able to digest food. That's why the vets have to get it out.'

‘That’s awful,’ Ollie said. ‘I knew littering was bad, but I didn’t really think that it ends up in the water. Or that it could kill animals.’

Sophia sighed and turned back to watch Kartika.

Ollie was just about to get them all some water, when Sophia noticed Marwa leaning closer to the monitor.

‘Is everything okay?’ Sophia asked.

‘I’m not sure,’ Marwa said. ‘I need a second opinion. Could you see if Lauren and your mum are finished in surgery, Soph?’ She turned back to Kartika, chewing the end of her pencil. ‘She looks uncomfortable. Something definitely isn’t right.’

Chapter 12

Cub concern!

'Back soon,' Sophia called, racing out the door.

She spotted Lani heading into a room. Sophia's mum and Lauren were both there, stripping off plastic gloves and washing their hands.

Jackpot!

'Marwa needs you,' Sophia said.

Lauren dried her hands quickly and headed out the door. 'What's happened?'

Sophia was almost skipping to keep up. 'Kartika might be trying to birth the third cub, but Marwa said she's looking uncomfortable.'

They raced into the observation room. Ollie was looking as worried as Marwa. The other tiger keeper, Brad, was there now too. Lauren and Donna joined them at the monitor.

'What's going on?' Ollie asked in a hushed voice.

Everyone was talking so quietly Sophia and Ollie couldn't hear their words. But there was no missing the tension.

Donna's face was serious when she guided Sophia and Ollie to the back of the room.

'Mum, what's happing?' Sophia asked quietly.

'This next cub's taking a bit too long,' she said. 'So we're going to get everything ready in case we need to jump in and help.'

Ollie and Sophia frowned and exchanged a quick look. They knew getting involved when an animal was having a baby would only happen in a real emergency.

'We hope that won't be needed,' Donna continued, 'but I'm going to get your dad to pick you up.'

'No–'

Sophia stopped talking as her mum raised her hand. 'Please, Soph. Don't argue. He'll drop you home too, Ollie.'

Sophia looked at the floor, then back at her mum.

'Please let us stay. We won't be distracting.'

'I know.' She gave Sophia a hug. 'But I can't be worrying about getting you two home if this goes late. It's the end of the day so we're light on staff as it is.'

'Then let us help,' Sophia said.

Eddie appeared in the doorway. Waddle was tucked inside a pouch cradled in his arms. 'Lani said you need me, Lauren?'

Lauren slapped her forehead. 'Oh, I forgot you had the joey. I needed you on standby for the tiger cubs if we need to help Kartika.'

'We could look after Waddle,' Sophia said quickly.

'Yeah,' Ollie said. 'We've fed echidna puggles and a koala joey before.'

'And Eddie already taught me to make up the food,' Sophia said proudly.

Lauren and Donna looked at Eddie.

He gave a little nod.

'That could work,' Donna said. 'Eddie, will you get them set up through there?' She pointed at a small room joined to the one they were in by a glass door.

Sophia squealed and threw her arms around her mum and then Lauren.

'We won't let you down,' Ollie said.

Then everyone was moving.

Sophia could hardly believe her mum had agreed. They were getting to be real vet assistants. It was a dream come true. She just wished the reason wasn't trouble with Kartika and her cubs.

Ollie suddenly didn't look so happy. He sat down, head in his hands. 'Do you really think they'll operate on Kartika, Eddie?' he asked, looking up.

'I don't know,' Eddie said. 'But we need

to stay positive. There's a risk, but they'll do their best to make sure mum and cub are both okay.'

Ollie let out a breath and nodded.

Eddie gently lowered the wrapped-up wombat joey into Ollie's lap.

'Keep your hands cupped around the edges,' Eddie said. 'If she wiggles, it's okay to let her poke her head out.' He nodded at Ollie. 'Just like that. You're doing great. She's due for a feed soon,' he said. 'Soph, are you on that?'

She nodded. 'I know what to do.'

Sophia went to the bench where Eddie had set up what she needed for the food.

She could feel her heart pounding as she carefully weighed the formula. Then taking a deep breath she transferred it to a container, being careful not to spill even a tiny bit. Sophia knew how important this was and how they were trusting her to get it right.

Once she had added the special milk powder and water, she exhaled. She'd done it.

Eddie was smiling. 'I can tell Waddle is in good hands. I've got to get ready, just in case. But I'll be just next door.' Eddie gave them one last nod, then headed out of the room.

His footsteps had barely faded away

when Ollie sucked in a breath.

'She's wiggling,' he said.

Soph pulled back the pouch. Two big ears popped out, then the tiny fur-covered head.

'Just keep calm and still, Ollie,' Sophia said. 'Being near the heat of your body will keep her happy. You're the perfect heater.'

Sophia carefully took the mixture and transferred it to a little bottle.

When she handed it to Ollie, Waddle didn't need any encouraging.

'She's so hungry,' Ollie said.

The only sound was a tiny *slurp*, *slurp*, *slurp* as they watched Waddle drink.

When she was done, Ollie wrapped her back up in the pouch.

They were feeling tired now and worried about Kartika, so neither of them said much as the minutes ticked by. Minutes turned into an hour.

Sophia's tummy growled. 'I'm even hungrier than Waddle was,' she said.

Suddenly Ollie's head jerked up. 'What was that?'

'I'll check.' Sophia stood up but before she had the chance to look into the next room, Eddie strode through the door, followed closely by Sophia's mum.

They were both grinning.

'Kartika did it,' Donna said. 'She's just given birth to the third cub and they're all doing fine. No help needed!'

Sophia's eyes filled with tears of relief.

Ollie let out a huge breath. 'Three more Sumatran tigers in the world,' he said.

'And now it's definitely time for you two to go home,' Donna said, smiling.

This time, they didn't argue.

Chapter 13

New arrivals

It was only just light when Max pulled into the Zoo carpark.

Ollie yawned loudly.

Donna had stayed at the hospital until late so she was having a sleep in. Max had offered to pick Sophia up and drive them both in for their volunteering duties. The only problem was, he had a *really* early start.

Sophia's dad had come in to wake her

up while it was still dark.

'Thanks for the lift, Max,' Sophia said, rubbing her tired eyes.

First stop was the Wildlife Hospital. They checked in on the little seal who was awake, doing well and was incredibly cute.

'When you're released, try to stay away from the plastic stuff,' Ollie whispered.

Then they found Brad on monitor duty keeping an eye on Kartika and the three cubs curled up in the nursing box.

Sophia and Ollie watched for a while as the tiny, fluffy cubs squirmed and wriggled in the hay. Kartika gave them an occasional lick. One little cub shuffled over to its mum for some breakfast.

Ollie's stomach growled.

'Everyone's hungry,' Brad said, laughing.

'We'd better go and find Pixie,' Sophia said. 'She said to meet her at the chimpanzees.'

It was cool and quiet as they made their way along the path from the Wildlife Hospital. They looked out at the harbour as they walked. The boats were still and the water was calm.

When they got to the chimpanzee habitat, Sophia automatically looked for Lisa. With her pregnant belly, she was usually easy to spot, but not today.

Where was she?

Sophia grabbed Ollie's arm.

'Look!' she pointed at a spot in front of a tall climbing frame.

'What am I looking at?' Ollie asked, squinting.

'Lisa,' Sophia said, 'AND her baby.'

'Her . . .' Ollie's eyes opened with surprise. 'Oh, wow.'

'Quick! Let's go find a keeper,' Sophia said.

They sprinted back towards the hospital, only to find Pixie striding towards them.

In one hand Pixie held a tray of reusable cups and, in the other, a paper bag.

'Pixie,' Sophia called out. 'It's so exciting! Lisa's had her baby!'

'That's amazing,' Pixie said. 'Show me.'

They turned and walked as fast they could back to the habitat. Pixie carefully balancing the drinks.

'Another baby to add to our Zoo family,' she said. 'It's been quite a night. How does it feel to be the first to see our newest addition?'

Sophia's heart felt close to bursting. 'It's beyond incredible,' she said.

Ollie nodded. 'The baby looks like a hairy human baby with huge ears! They do share ninety-nine percent of the same DNA as us, I guess.'

Pixie put down the bag and drinks and unclipped her radio, calling up to the Wildlife Hospital to share the news. Sophia smiled as she heard a cheer through the speaker.

Lisa was wandering around, the little baby snuggling close to her belly.

'When will the keepers know if it's a boy or girl?' Sophia asked Pixie.

'It's going to be a while before we know much about it,' Pixie said.

'Lisa will be very protective of her little one. But from what I can see, Mum's doing a great job.'

Sophia, Ollie and Pixie settled on a timber seat opposite the chimpanzee habitat.

'I nearly forgot!' Pixie said. 'Hot chocolates!' She handed one each to Sophia and Ollie. 'Well, they'll probably be cool chocolates by now. And . . . ta da!'

A delicious smell wafted towards Sophia as Pixie opened the bag. Her stomach rumbled. 'Bacon and egg rolls. My absolute favourite,' Sophia said.

Pixie handed one to Ollie too.

'Does this one have–'

'Barbecue sauce?' Pixie said. 'Of course.'

Ollie grinned. 'You're the best.'

'I know,' Pixie said, taking a big bite of her roll.

No one spoke as they ate their breakfast – gooey, runny egg dripping down their hands.

Sophia sipped her drink, feeling light and happy.

Ollie leaned back and patted his stomach. 'Thanks so much, Pixie.'

'My pleasure,' she said. 'Hey, you're my fact guy, Ollie. Tell me – what do baby apes sleep in?'

Ollie's eyes narrowed. There was something not serious in Pixie's voice and the cheeky grin on her face gave her away.

'I don't know,' he said. 'What *do* baby apes sleep in?'

'*Ape*-ri-cots.'

Pixie cracked up laughing.

'That was genuinely bad,' Sophia said. 'Like, really bad.'

That set Pixie off again. Her laughter was infectious. Sophia started to giggle too, and once she started she couldn't stop. Soon Ollie was laughing as well.

Chapter 14

Tiny dragons

Not even Fred the brush turkey's mission to put the garden everywhere except in the garden could dampen Sophia and Ollie's good mood. Today they only had to rake and scoop the mulch and then they were free.

'What do you want to do when we're finished?' Sophia asked.

Suddenly Ollie was very focussed on the leaves he was scooping up.

‘What’s wrong?’ Sophia asked.

‘Well, I’m a bit worried you’ll be cross,’ he said, very quietly, shuffling his feet. ‘We’re looking after Katy again today.’

‘That’s awesome,’ Sophia said.

Ollie’s head snapped up. ‘Really?’

‘Of course,’ Sophia said, and she really, truly meant it.

After finishing their work, they headed towards the Backyard Team shed.

‘Good morning, you two.’ Jason the reptile keeper was striding towards them from the Wildlife Hospital.

‘Hi,’ Ollie said. ‘How are the bearded dragon eggs?’

‘They’re hatching!’ Jason said. ‘I’m just on my way back there. Want to come and see?’

Sophia grinned at Ollie who was

nodding enthusiastically.

Jason led them into the back area of the reptile house where eggs were placed carefully in a special incubator that looked like a small fridge. One of the eggs looked collapsed, like it had all the air sucked out.

'What happened to that egg?' Sophia said, suddenly worried. 'Did it get squashed?'

'No. That one just hatched.' Jason pointed. 'See.'

A little bearded dragon was sitting still and quiet on the bottom of a habitat close by.

'It's so tiny,' Ollie said. 'No bigger than my thumb.'

'I've just finished the first weigh and measure. It's crazy to think in a year they'll be more than thirty centimetres long,'

Jason said. 'Maybe bigger if they're boys.'

'Look!' said Ollie.

In the incubator, a tiny dragon head was poking out of another egg.

Ollie and Sophia watched as the baby bearded dragon wiggled and squirmed until it managed to get all the way out.

'Oh, hello!' Sophia said. 'You look exhausted.'

'Hatching is really tiring,' Jason explained. 'It's not uncommon for a dragon to rest for up to a day with only its head out of the shell. You were lucky to see one get free so quickly. What are you two up to now?'

'We're going to meet Pixie and Katy up at the gift shop,' Sophia said.

'Can I recommend you take a little detour via nguwing nura – Nocturnal Country?' Jason suggested.

'Why?' Ollie asked.

'I don't want to spoil the surprise!' he said with a smile.

Sophia and Ollie quickly said goodbye to Jason and the dragons and raced up the main path.

Stepping into the dark of nguwing nura – Nocturnal Country always felt like entering another world.

The only sounds were the chirps and whistles of birds and the trickling sound of water. It was cool and quiet, and so calm and peaceful.

Ahead, a few people were staring into a pool of water. Sophia recognised most of them, including one of their favourite keepers, Kate.

Kate stepped aside to make room for Ollie and Sophia. 'Take a look,' she said. 'We have a very special addition due to make her public debut today.'

Sophia and Ollie peered into the dark water.

'Over there,' Ollie said, pointing to where a small waterfall trickled into the pond.

Sophia saw it too. A sleek little shape was moving under the water, gliding near some tree roots. Suddenly, a little head with a distinctive duck bill popped up.

'It's Tilly!' Sophia exclaimed.

Kate grinned. 'She looks very pleased with her new habitat. She's been flipping, diving and swimming around. I'm glad we named her after the Matildas football team. She's got such a fighting spirit!'

'She was only a puggle when they found her, wasn't she?' Ollie said.

Kate nodded. 'Pretty much – about four months old. She was so unwell, malnourished and covered in ticks.'

'I thought a puggle was a baby echidna,' Sophia said.

'It is,' Kate explained. 'But it's also what we call a baby platypus. Although, sometimes we call them platypups.'

'Ha,' Ollie exclaimed. 'Platypup! I like that. When there's more than one platypus, they're called a paddle of platypuses.'

'Probably because of the shape of their tails,' Sophia suggested. 'It's perfect.'

Ollie and Sophia spent the rest of the walk planning where they'd take Katy.

When Pixie met them outside the Zoo shop, Katy was being piggybacked. She was trying to hide, but she was wearing a huge pair of furry ears attached to a headband.

Sophia giggled. 'Nice ears, Pixie.'

'It's ME!' Katy called out, sticking her head around Pixie's shoulder. Pixie put her down.

Katy hopped straight over to Ollie for a hug.

'Why don't we go to see the baby kangas first,' Ollie said. 'Katy's certainly dressed the part.'

He caught his sister mid-hop, and they all headed into the Zoo.

Chapter 15

A surprise baby

'Hey, Soph. What do you get if you cross a kangaroo with an alien?' Pixie's eyes were open comically wide. 'A Mars-upial.'

Sophia giggled. 'I actually like that one,' she said.

They were sitting in buru nura – Kangaroo Country, surrounded by emus and wallabies and kangaroos.

'I've got one for you,' Sophia said.

'What do stylish kangaroos wear?'

Pixie looked surprised. 'You're telling *me* a joke?' she said. 'I don't know. What do they wear?'

'Jumpsuits.'

Pixie howled with laughter. 'I've finally converted you to the bad joke club,' she said.

One of the joeys hopped closer to them, sniffing at Pixie's knee and an emu wandered up, poking its head over her shoulder.

'Oh, hello there,' said Pixie. 'Did you all like the jokes too?'

'Soph. Pixie. Come over here,' Ollie called out. 'Katy's found something.'

Ollie was crouching down, holding Katy's hand. He was looking closely at one of the larger kangaroos.

'Is something wrong?' Pixie asked.

She squatted beside him.

'Well, I'm not sure,' he said. 'There are three new joeys, and they're all out of the pouches. Right?'

Pixie nodded. 'Yes, that's right.'

Sophia looked around. 'They're over there, and there and there,' she said, pointing at them.

Ollie raised his eyebrows. 'Then who is this?'

A little furry head, with too-big ears and tiny black eyes was peeking out from the kangaroo pouch in front of them.

Sophia crouched down beside Ollie and Katy. The joey was so small and so cute, much smaller and younger than the others.

Katy giggled as the joey disappeared briefly then popped its head back out.

She covered her eyes, then uncovered them. 'Peek-a-boo,' she said, giggling again.

'It's a surprise baby!' said Pixie, her face lighting up.

'Just like you, Katy,' Ollie said with a grin. 'Mum says you were a surprise. And you're a lot younger than me too.'

Pixie laughed. 'Well, I think that's a bit different,' she said. 'This is a "paused pregnancy". Kangaroos and wallabies have two eggs ready to develop into babies, then the mum puts one on hold until after the first baby is born. They might even pause the pregnancy longer if the environment isn't great. The technical name is embryonic diapause.'

Pixie jumped up and they heard her talking excitedly to Bethany, one of the macropod keepers.

'Well done, Katy,' said Sophia. 'You're a natural zookeeper!'

Katy looked up and started to hop around like a kangaroo.

Ollie smiled. 'She might have to figure out that she's not an animal first.'

Sophia and Ollie followed Katy as

she explored, crouching beside rocks, or peering into bushes and under trees.

'It's amazing how many babies have been born,' Ollie said, watching a little joey hop past.

'Yeah,' Sophia said. 'And how many we've got to see and help. This has been the most exciting week ever.'

'Totally,' Ollie agreed. 'We got to help the baby goats and shower a baby pygmy hippo.'

'Feed the meerkat pups and little Waddle the wombat,' Sophia said.

'Plus we were the first to see Lisa's baby and we watched a bearded dragon hatching.' Ollie was counting things off on his fingers. 'Now there's the surprise joey, and we saw . . .'

'Kartika's cubs being born!' Sophia and Ollie said together.

Sophia sighed with happiness.

'I wonder how they're doing,' Ollie said. 'It's hard to imagine those little balls of fluff growing to be as big and strong as Kartika, isn't it? They like cute little kittens right now.'

'I know,' Sophia said. 'So, do you think the tiger cubs are the cutest babies in the Zoo?'

Ollie thought for a moment. 'I think so. How about you?'

Sophia thought about all the amazing baby animals she'd seen and helped that week.

Katy hopped by, making little *snick snick snick* noises like a kangaroo.

'It's a tough choice,' Sophia said. 'They're all pretty adorable, but I think we might be looking at the cutest baby of them all right now.'

Ollie laughed.

'You know, Soph. I think you might be right.'

Ollie's FUN fact file

- Most baby reptiles have an 'egg tooth' that helps them crack open their egg from the inside.
- Mother platypuses sweat out milk to feed their little platypups, orangutan babies can drink their mum's milk for up to eight years and dolphins can drink their mum's milk underwater.
- Elephants are pregnant for almost two years, but frilled shark pregnancies go for three and a half years!
- Some baby elephants suck their trunks, just like human babies suck their thumbs.
- Tiger cubs are born blind and find their mum through scent.

- Giraffes give birth standing up so when their babies are born, they fall all the way to the ground!
- Thankfully for their mums, rhinos don't have a horn when they're born.
- Seahorse females pass the eggs on to the males and they give birth to around 200 or more babies each!
- Some fish dads carry the eggs around in their mouth until they hatch. It's called 'mouthbrooding'!
- Meerkat groups have 'babysitters' who look after all the pups and teach them everything they need to know.
- A newborn kangaroo is only the size of a jellybean at birth and stays in the pouch until around six months old.
- More than a hundred mammal species can pause their pregnancies (embryonic diapause), but scientists are still learning about how it happens!

TARONGA
CONSERVATION SOCIETY AUSTRALIA®

For the Wild

This book has the power to protect.

This series was created in partnership with Taronga Conservation Society Australia. Taronga is a not-for-profit organisation whose vision is to secure a shared future for wildlife and people.

Taronga has released more than 55,000 animals into the wild through its conservation breeding programs and rehabilitation at its two Wildlife Hospitals and contributes to more than sixty conservation programs, including seventeen recovery breeding programs.

So when you purchase this book, visit their two Zoos, stay overnight, donate, or participate in an unforgettable behind-the-scenes experience, you're saving wildlife and supporting critical conservation work here in Australia and around the world.

Thank you for being a supporter for the wild.

taronga.org.au

Kristin Darell is the acclaimed author of the Football Fever series with Football Australia. She has also worked as a journalist for major Australian news organisations and is the Program Manager for the Australian Children's Laureate Foundation. She lives on Sydney's northern beaches with her husband, two children, two dogs, pet snake and three-legged pygmy bearded dragon.

Laura Wood is originally from a small town in the north of Italy. She studied illustration in Melbourne, where she started her illustration career. She works in both commercial art and books for children. After a few years of travelling around the world, she now lives in Milan, Italy.